MARVEL SUPER HERO SQUAD™

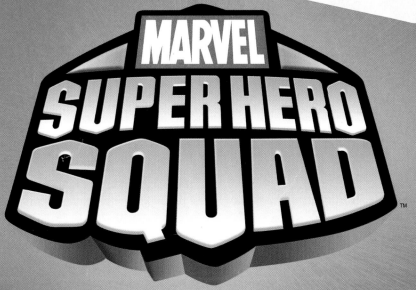

TM & © 2012 Marvel & Subs.

Little, Brown and Company

Hachette Book Group
237 Park Avenue, New York, NY 10017
Visit our website at www.lb-kids.com

LB kids is an imprint of Little, Brown and Company. The LB kids name and logo are trademarks of Hachette Book Group, Inc.

The publisher is not responsible for websites (or their content) that are not owned by the publisher.

First Edition: April 2012

ISBN 978-0-316-17859-4

Library of Congress Control Number: 2011935089

10 9 8 7 6 5 4 3 2 1

CW

Printed in the United States of America

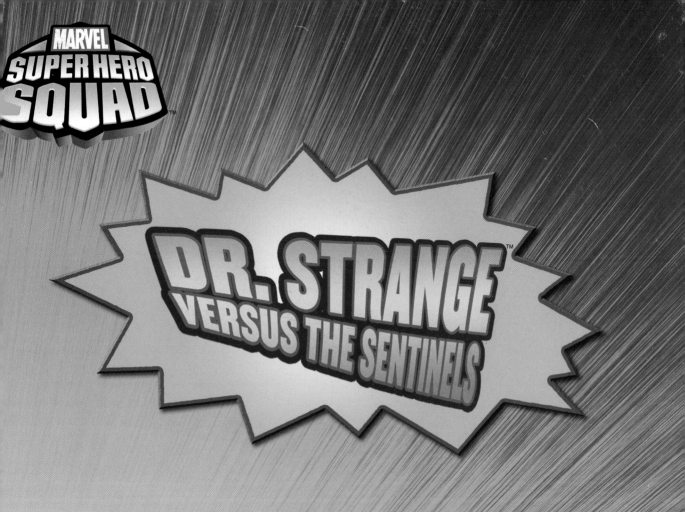

MARVEL SUPER HERO SQUAD™

DR. STRANGE™ VERSUS THE SENTINELS™

by Zachary Rau
illustrated by Guido Guidi

LITTLE, BROWN & COMPANY
LB kids

Inside Super Hero Squad headquarters, Dr. Strange and Mr. Fantastic study one of Dr. Doom's Sentinel robots.

Dr. Strange searches the astral plane for the energy that brings the robots to life.

Mr. Fantastic takes the Sentinel apart and puts it back together, hoping to discover how the robot works. He tries to jump-start the Sentinel with a burst of electricity.

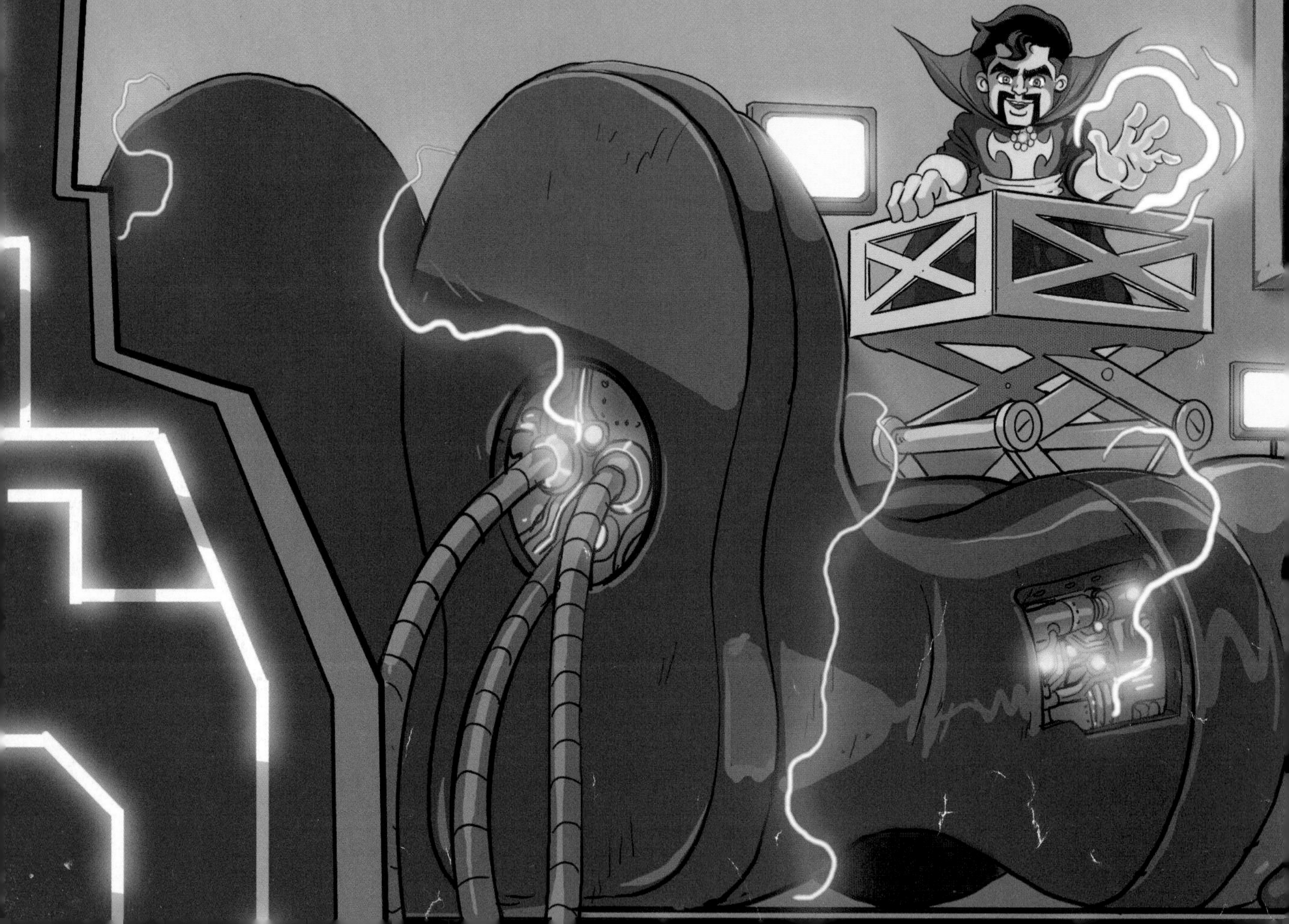

"You might want to step back, Strange," suggests Mr. Fantastic. "This could have shocking results."

"The only thing shocking is that you think this will have any effect at all," replies Dr. Strange.

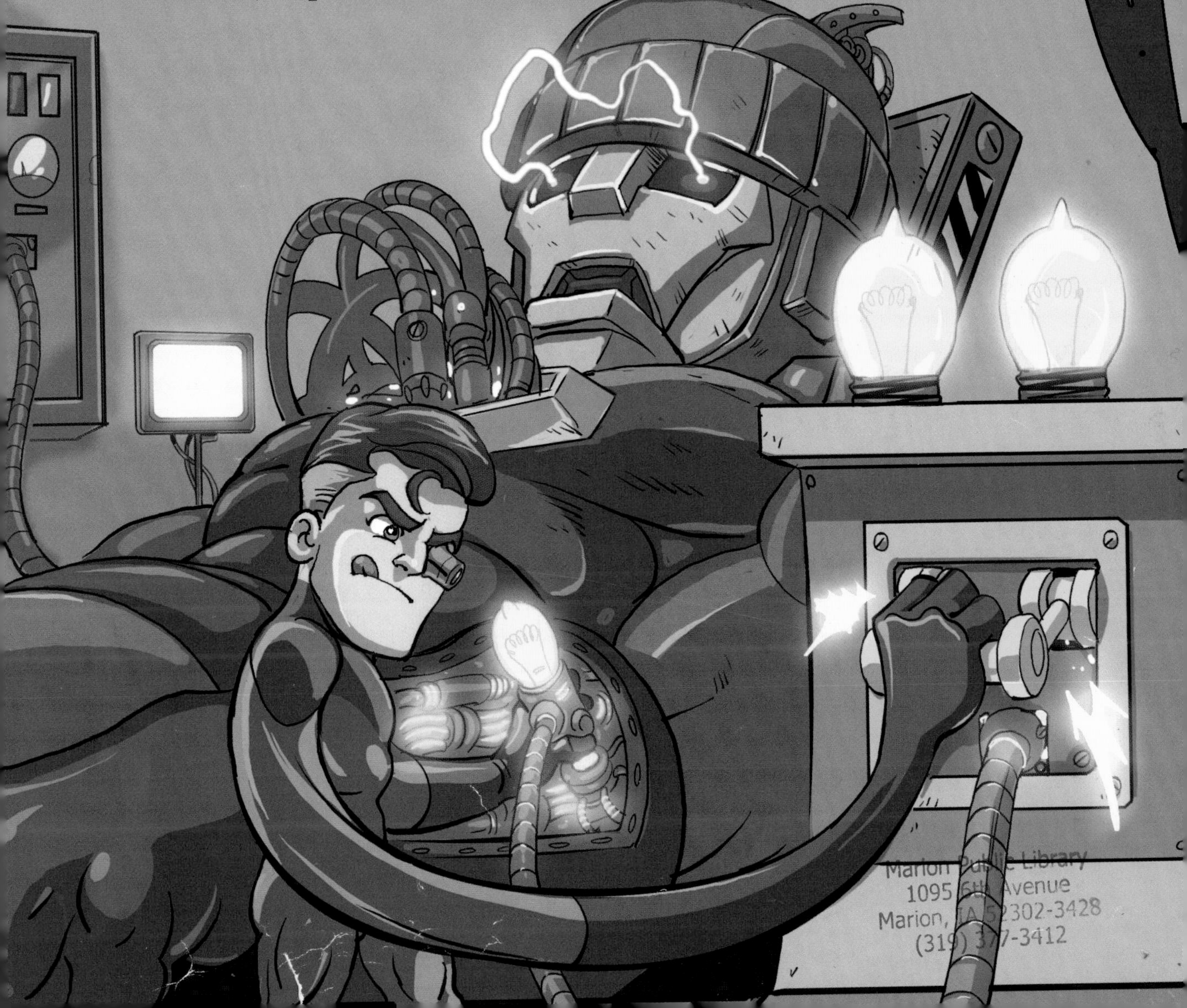

But Mr. Fantastic's test fizzles out. The Sentinel's electrical systems overload!

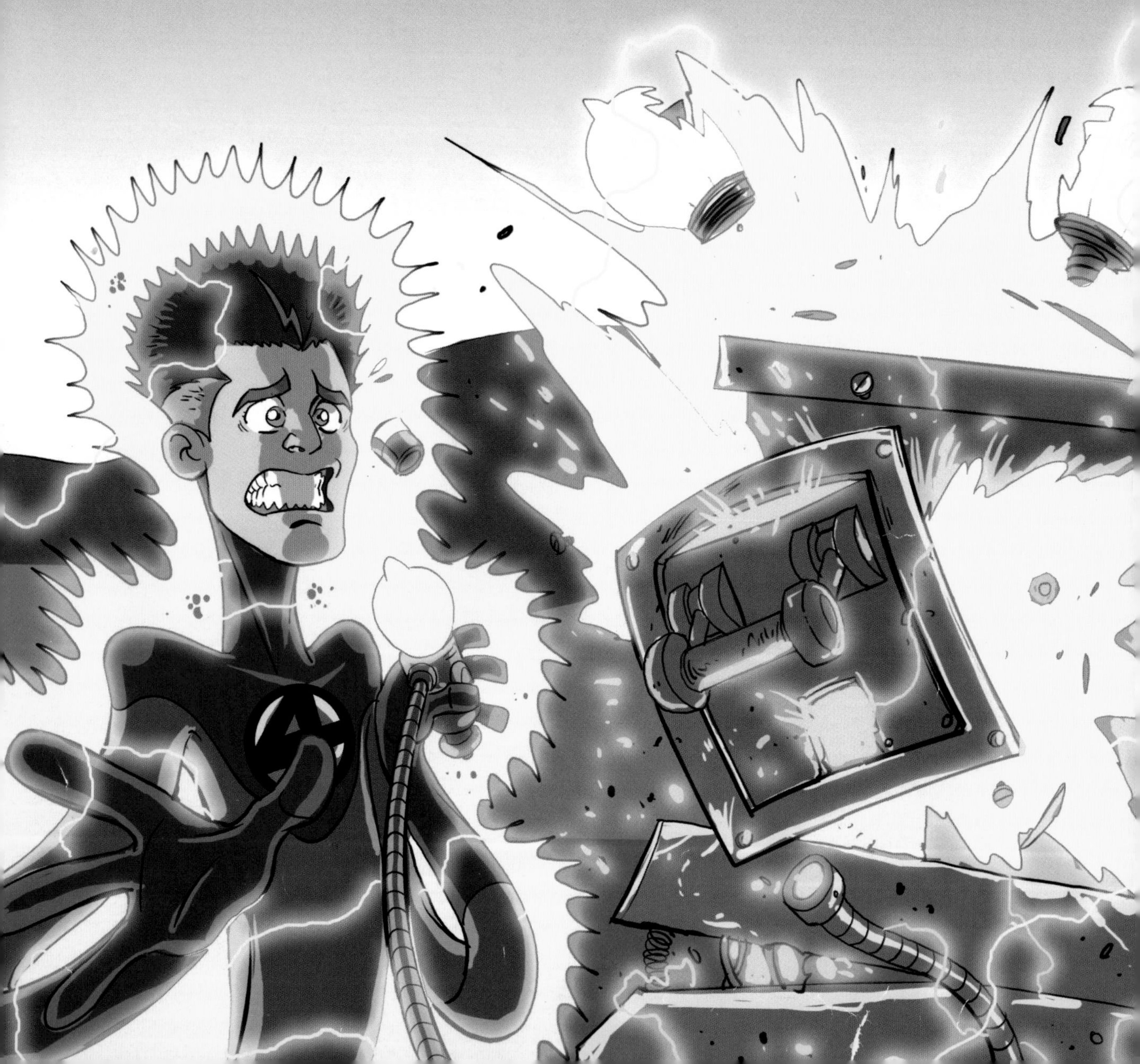

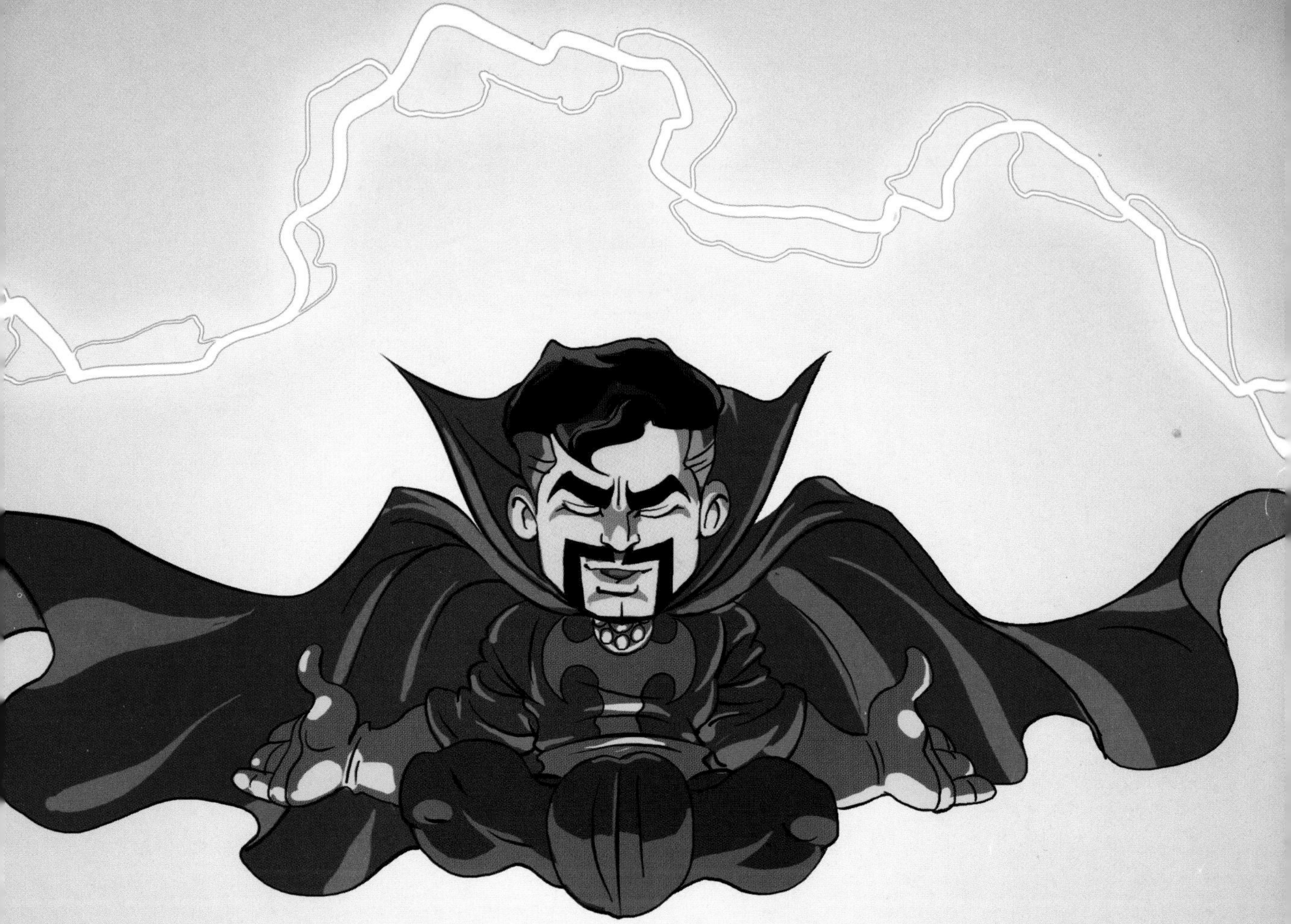

“Shocking, indeed,” quips Dr. Strange. “It seems this will require a more magical approach.” The mystic hero slips into a trance and begins to cast a spell. “In the name of the Eternal Vishanti,” he says as he begins to mutter an ancient language.

But his spell gets interrupted when Hulk suddenly stomps through the door of the lab!

"Hulk, I'm busy," Dr. Strange says with a groan as he falls to the floor and loses control of the spell.

"Doc, Hulk feel sick!" he complains. "Make Hulk better now!"

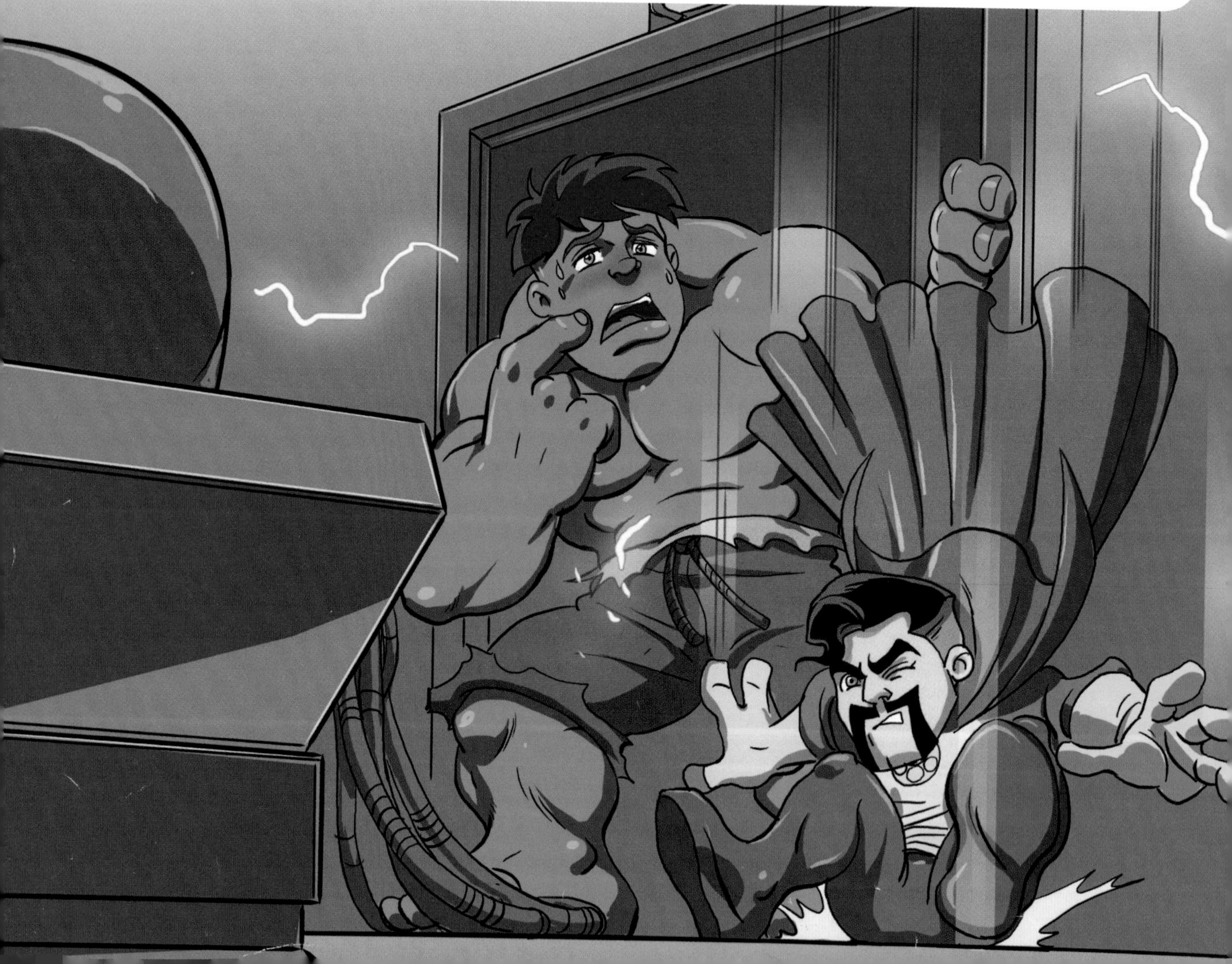

Uh-oh! The magic is out of control! The Sentinel emits a strange glow, and little cracks start to appear all over the robot, growing bigger and bigger, until the Sentinel bursts into hundreds of tiny pieces!

"Your way cracks me up!" teases Mr. Fantastic.

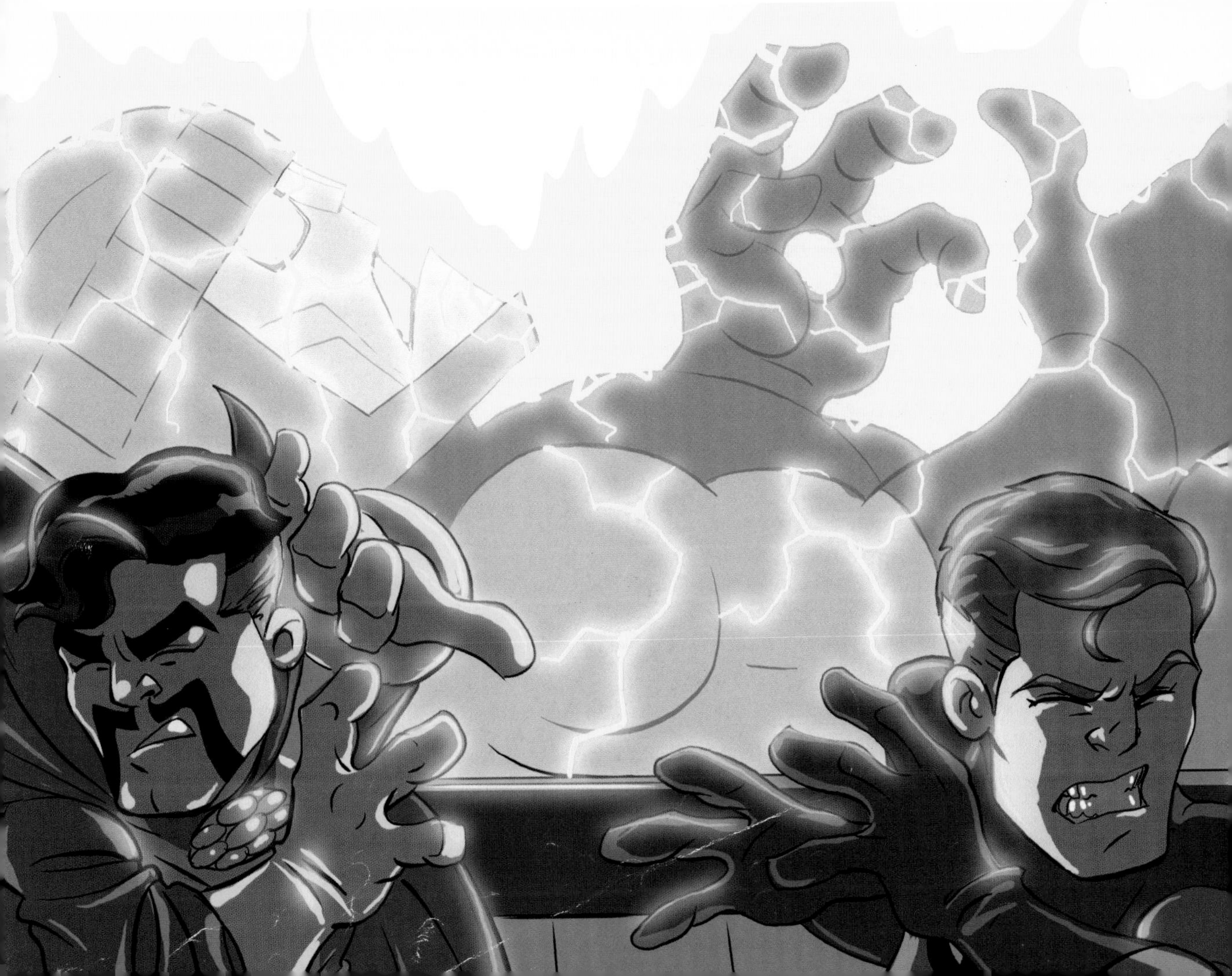

But wait! The Sentinel hasn't just broken into tiny pieces—it has splintered into tiny *Sentinels*! A swarm of insect-sized robots starts to buzz around the room.

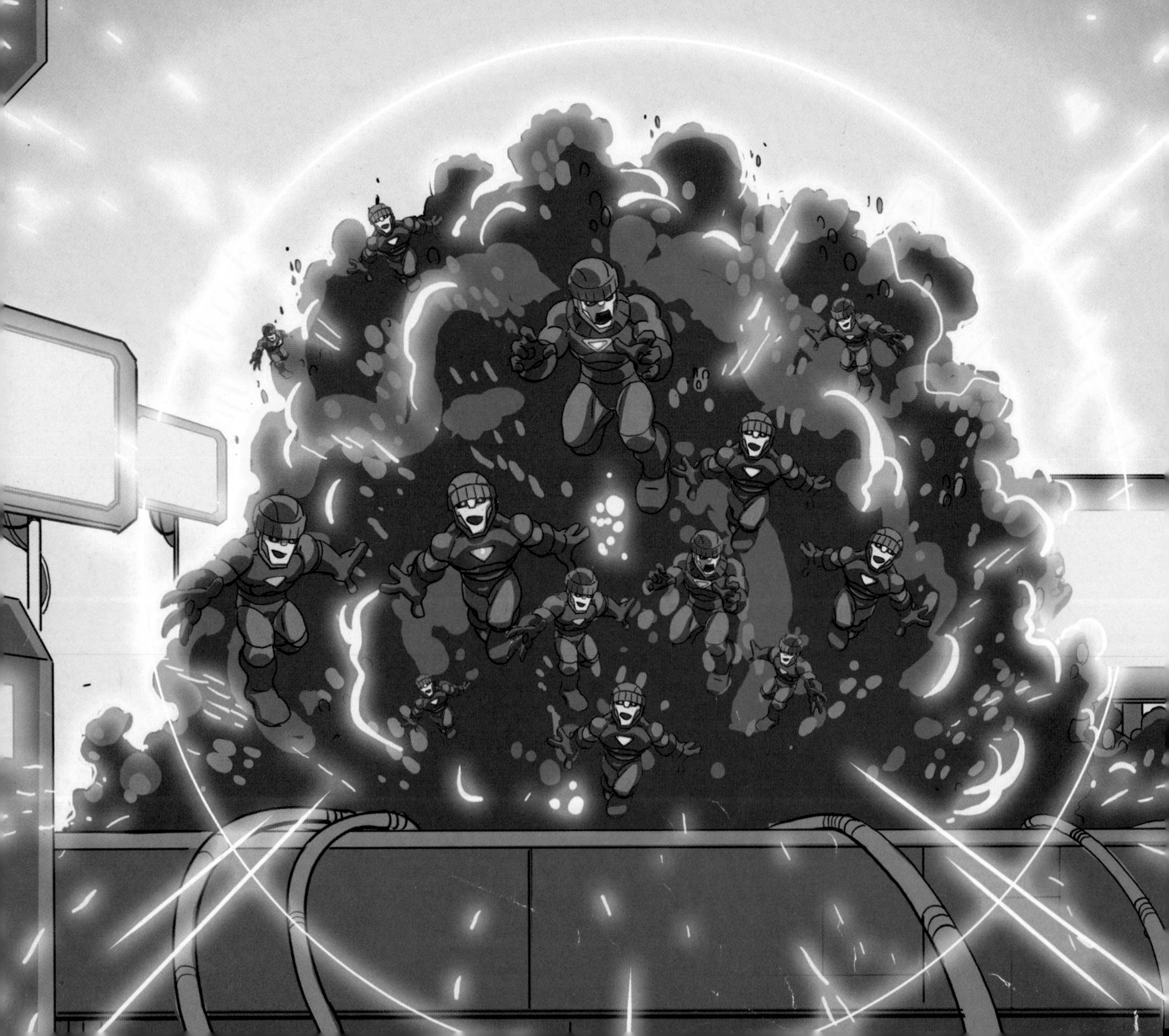

Dr. Strange and Mr. Fantastic jump into action. Dr. Strange runs over to a wall panel and pushes a large red button to lock the place down while Mr. Fantastic tries to contain the swarm.

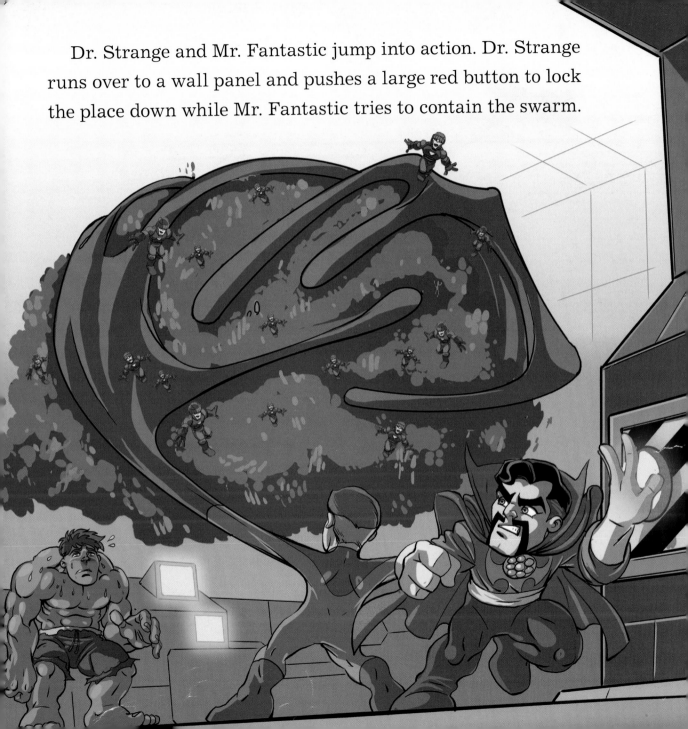

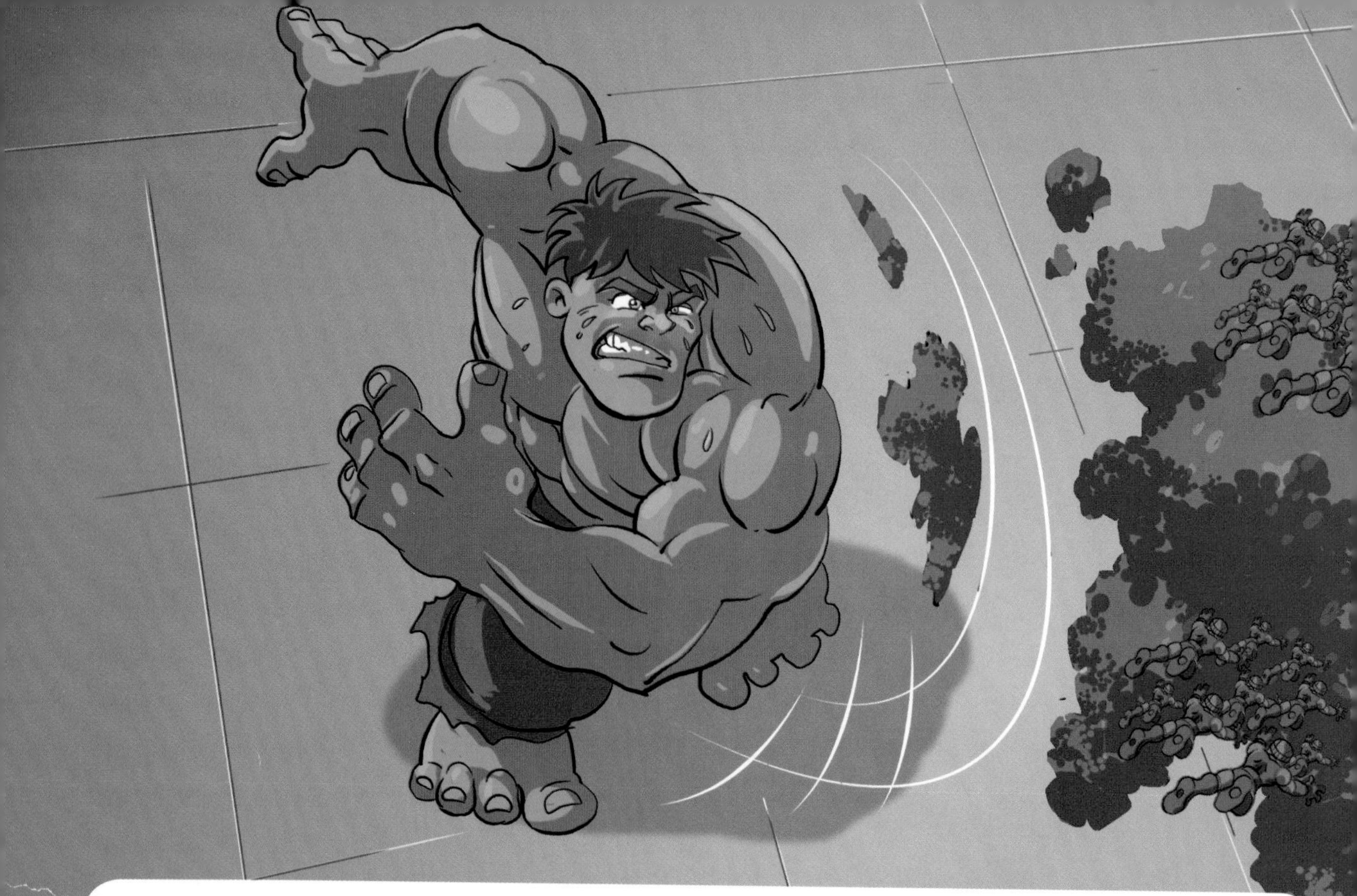

"Hulk hate bugs! Hulk hate being sick!" screams the green guy.

The giant Hulk swats at the swarm, scaring the tiny robots. One gets so scared that it flies past the heroes, out of the lab, and out of sight before the doors can close!

"Oh, no! Don't let them escape!" yells Mr. Fantastic. But the entire swarm is already following its leader out the door and down the hall.

"Instead of one problem, we now have hundreds!" cries Mr. Fantastic. "We need the whole Squad."

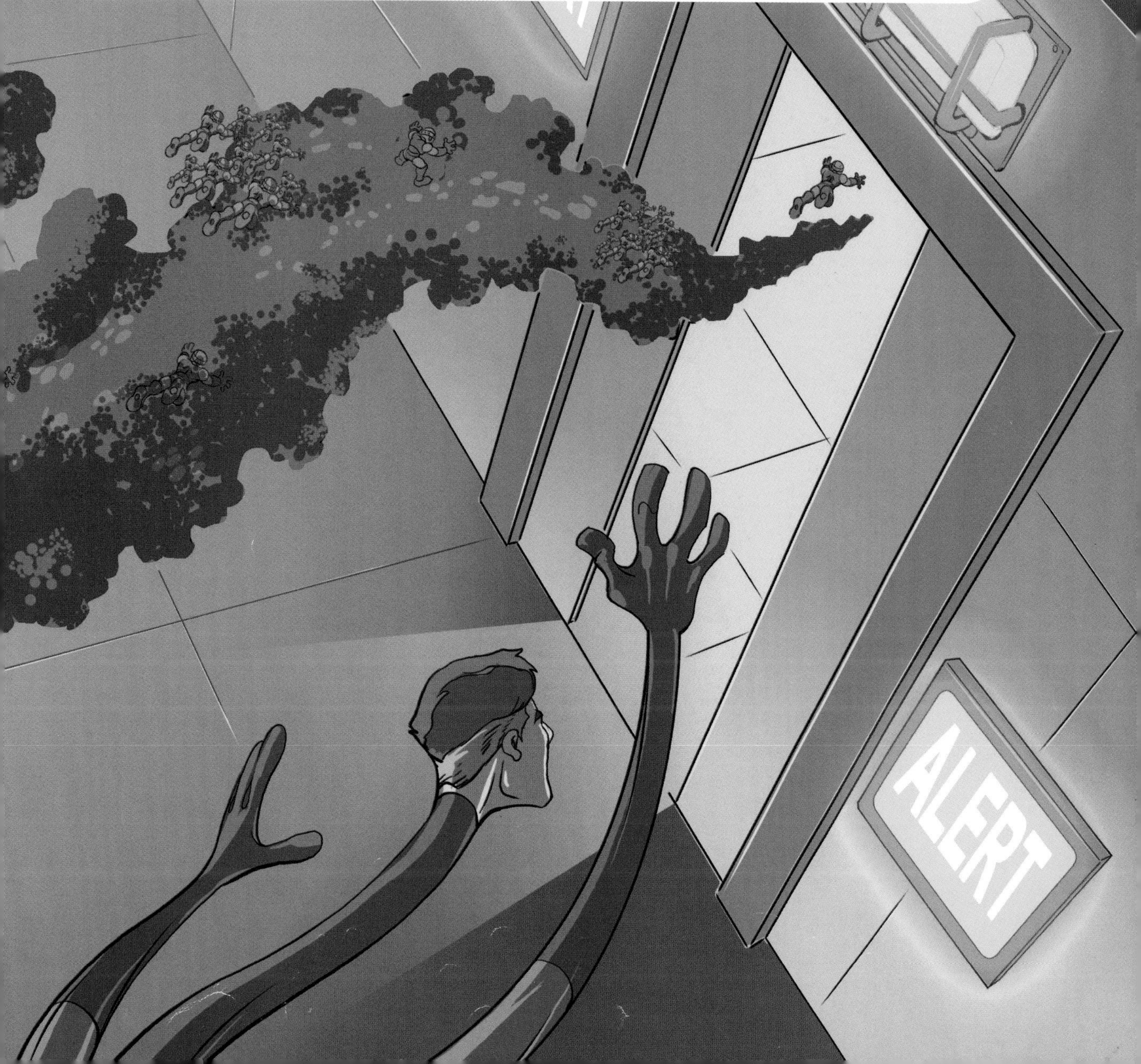
ALERT

More members of the Super Hero Squad quickly assemble.

"We have no choice. They are too small for the computer to detect easily. We're going to have to search each floor," explains Mr. Fantastic.

Captain America quickly directs the heroes. "Okay, break up into two teams, Squad! Let's find these things before they do any real damage. Or at least more than what Hulk has already caused today!"

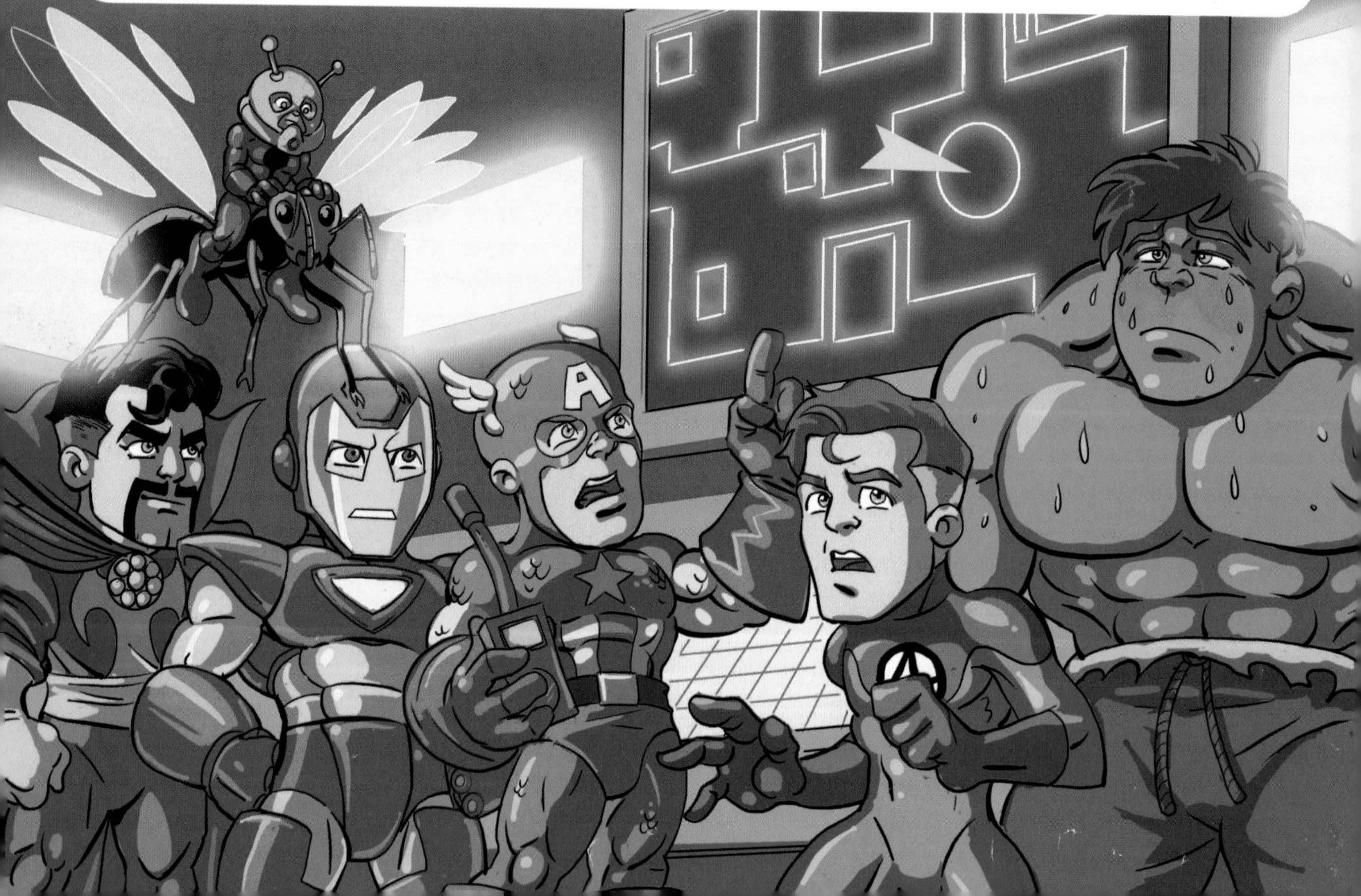

It isn't as hard to *find* the tiny Sentinels as it is to *catch* them.

"This is Team Two. We found the swarm near the armory," says Mr. Fantastic. "It looks like the robots have eaten through the control panel and are trying to get inside."

"We need to move now!" orders Captain America.

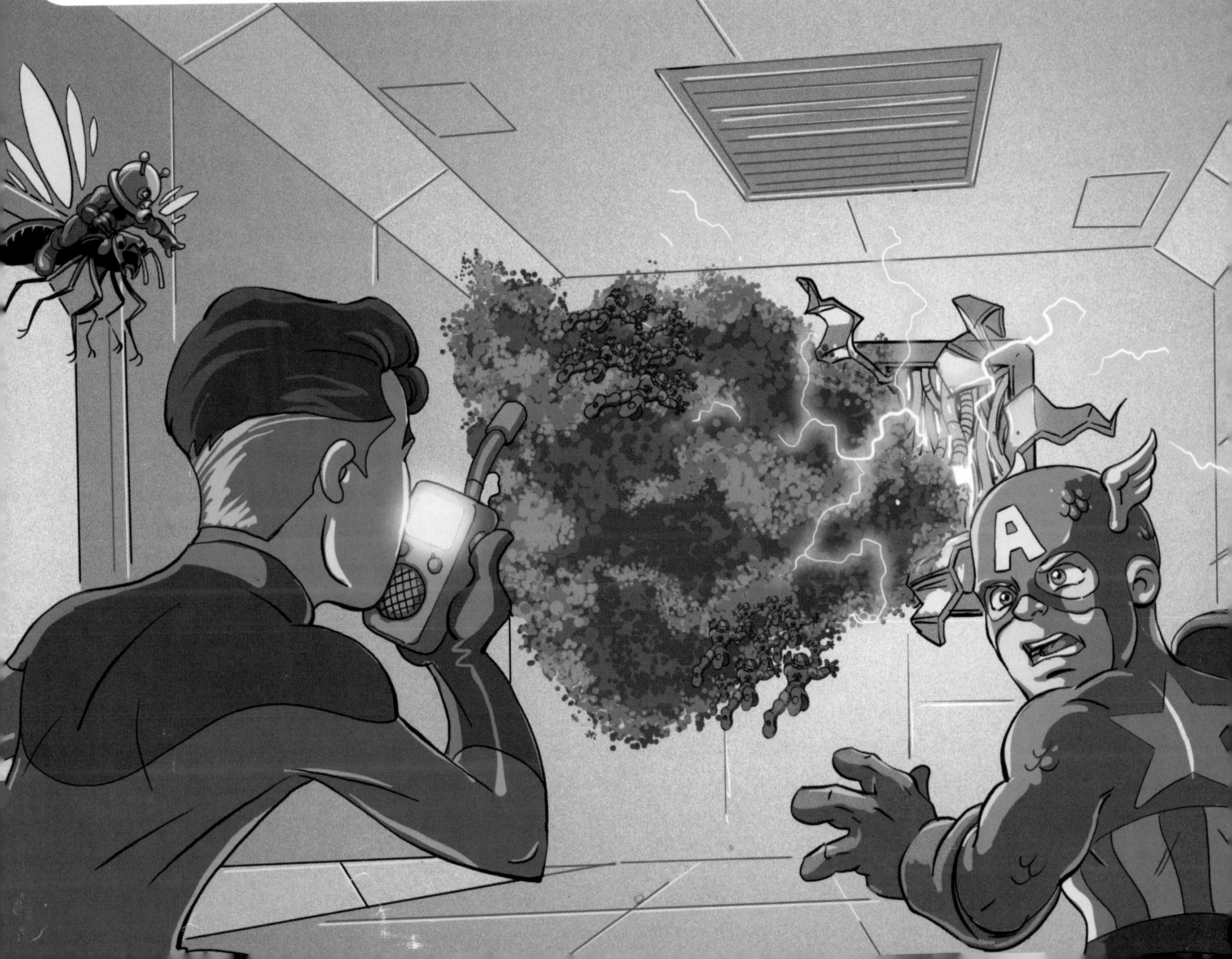

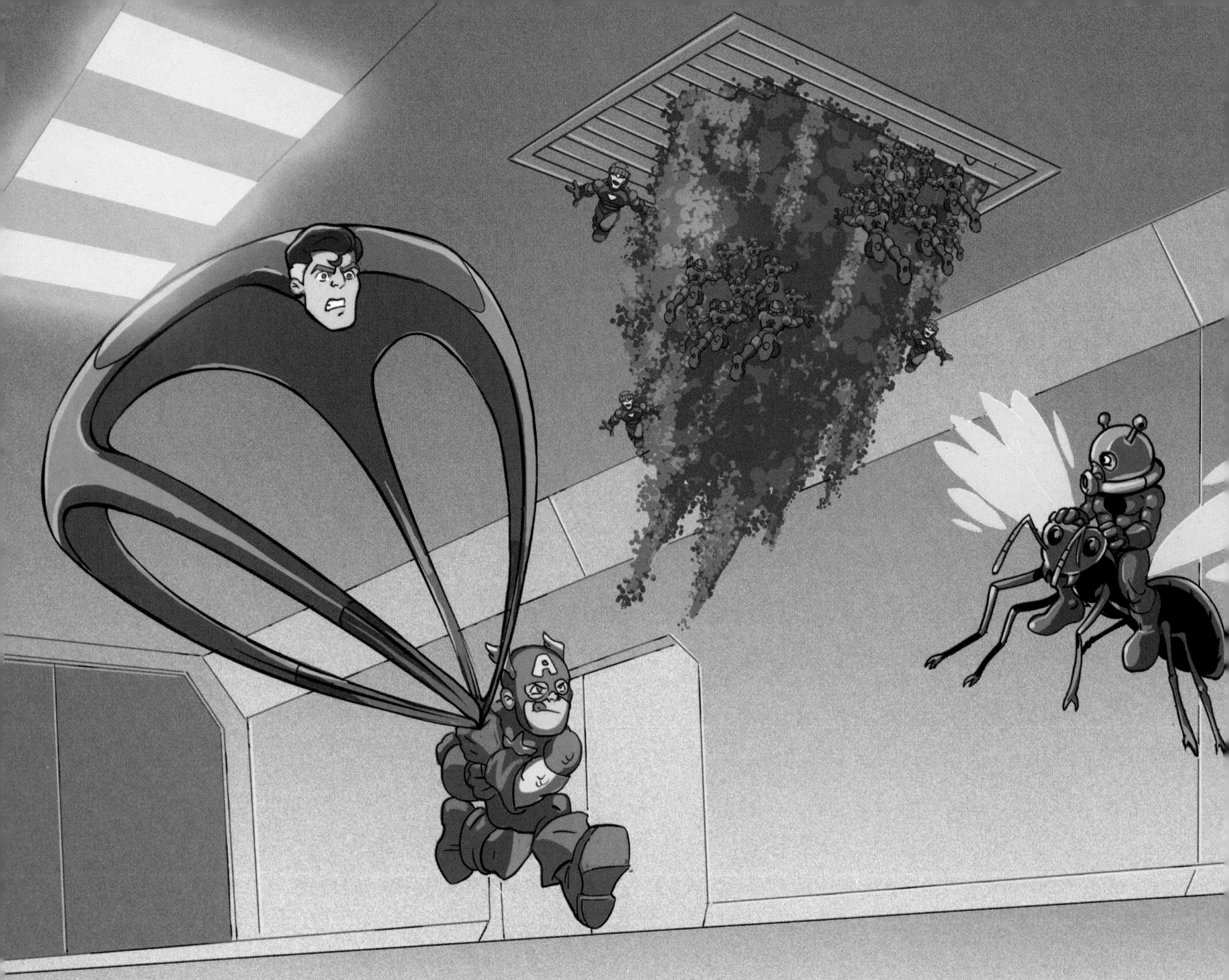

Captain America grabs Mr. Fantastic by the hands and feet and runs at the swarm, trying to use his friend's stretched body as a giant net. But the miniature Sentinels do not want to be caught! They are just too fast for the heroes. The robots fly into a vent above.

"Team One, this is Captain America. We lost them. They are in the vent, so keep your eyes peeled. Ant-Man is following."

The other team quickly picks up the trail. "The swarm is near the medical lab! I think it sees us," whispers Iron Man. "Hulk, scare it this way. Then, Strange, blast some of your magic stuff."

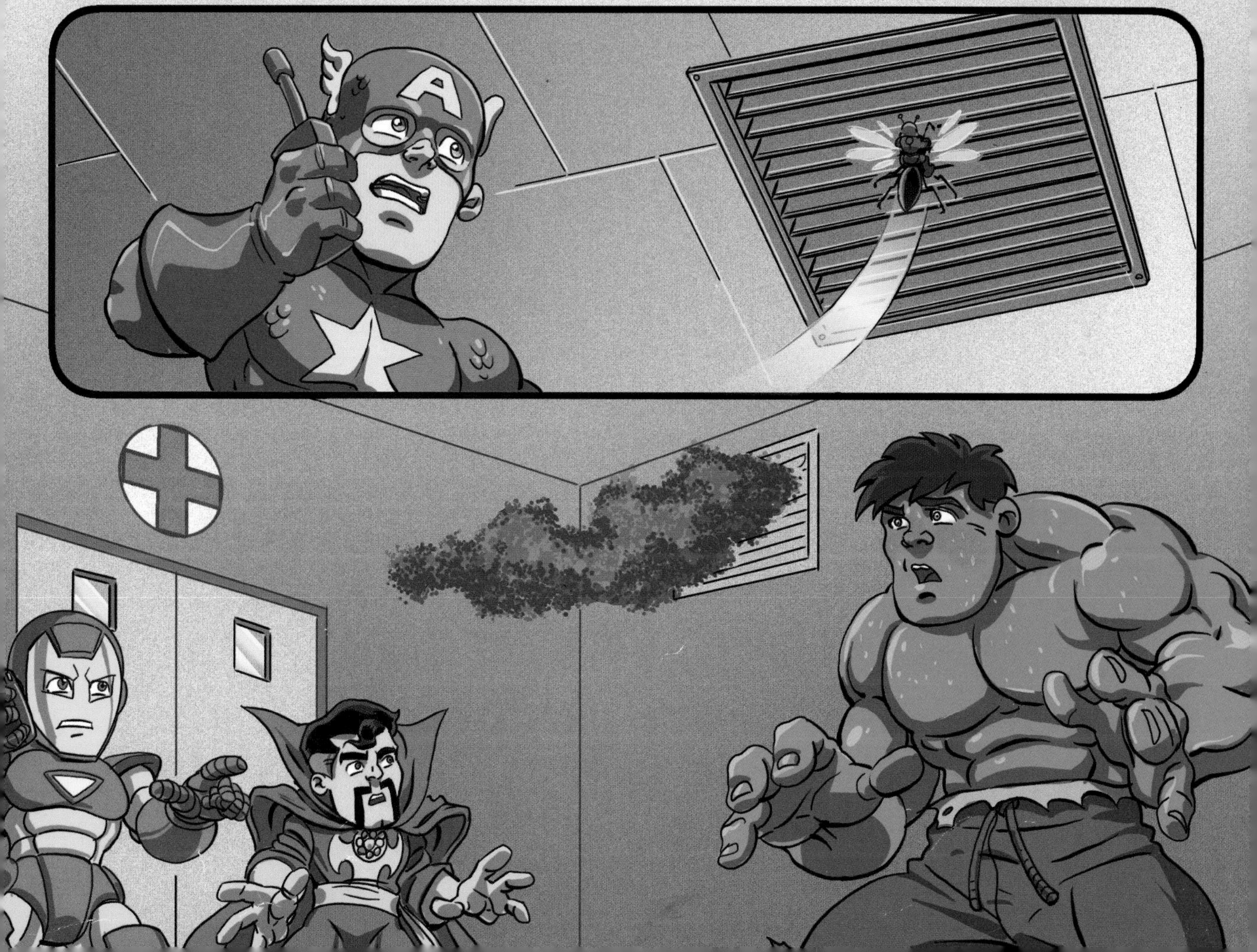

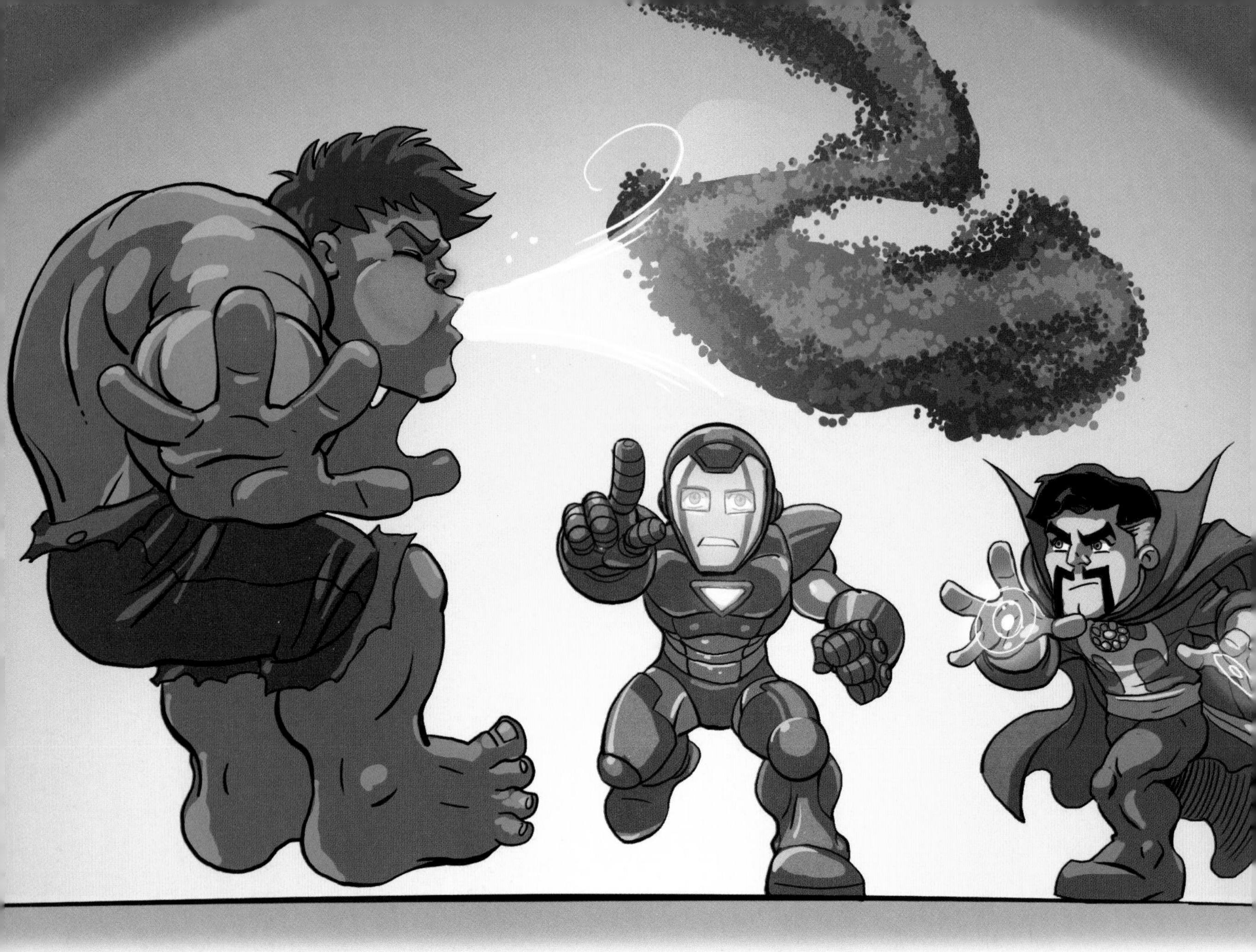

Suddenly, Hulk sneezes, startling the swarm and sending the machines zooming toward the other heroes.

"Yup, that is pretty scary," agrees Iron Man. "Good job, Hulk!"

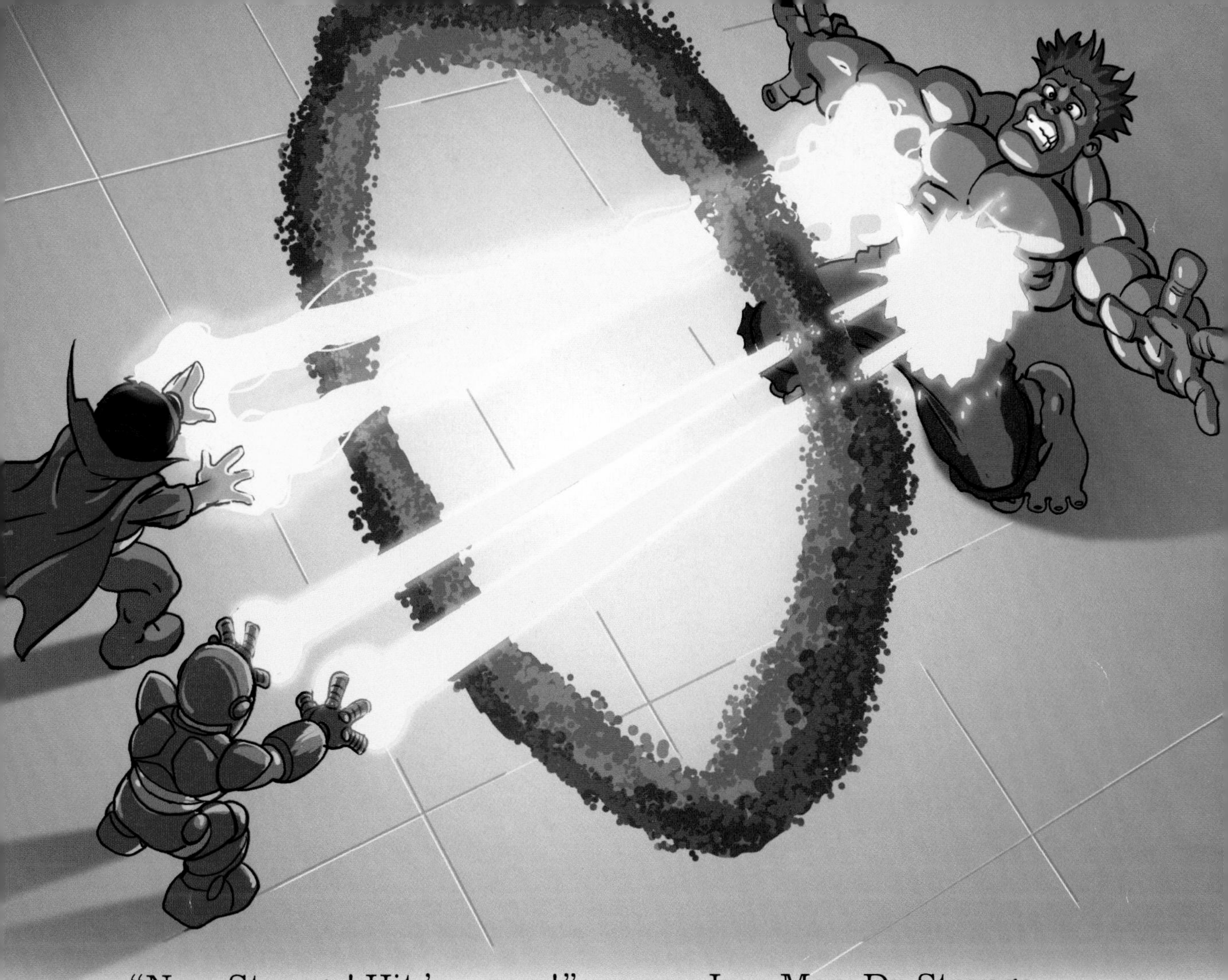

“Now, Strange! Hit ’em now!” screams Iron Man. Dr. Strange casts an ancient binding spell as Iron Man fires his lasers at the swarm.

Oops! The swarm dodges the heroes, and Hulk gets zapped!

"Captain America, Hulk is down, and Iron Man is following the swarm on his own into the medical lab!" Dr. Strange yells into his radio.

"We are on our way," replies Captain America.

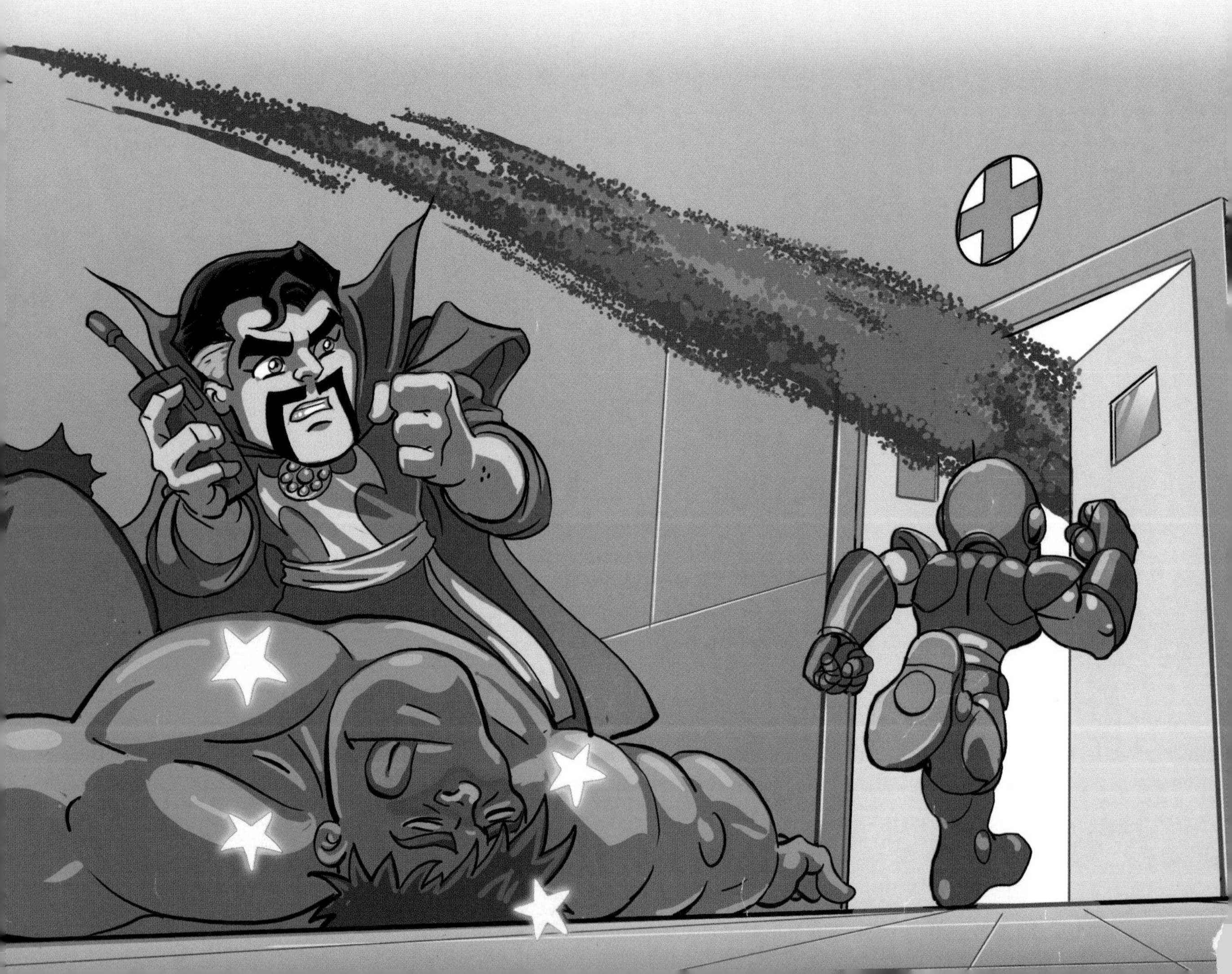

The rest of the Squad arrive, and they all race into the room to find Iron Man with the tiny Sentinels swirling happily around him.

"I tried to blast them, but they keep covering my eyes!" complains Iron Man. "They won't leave me alone!"

"Looks like you made some new friends," jokes Ant-Man. "They think you're their big robot dad!"

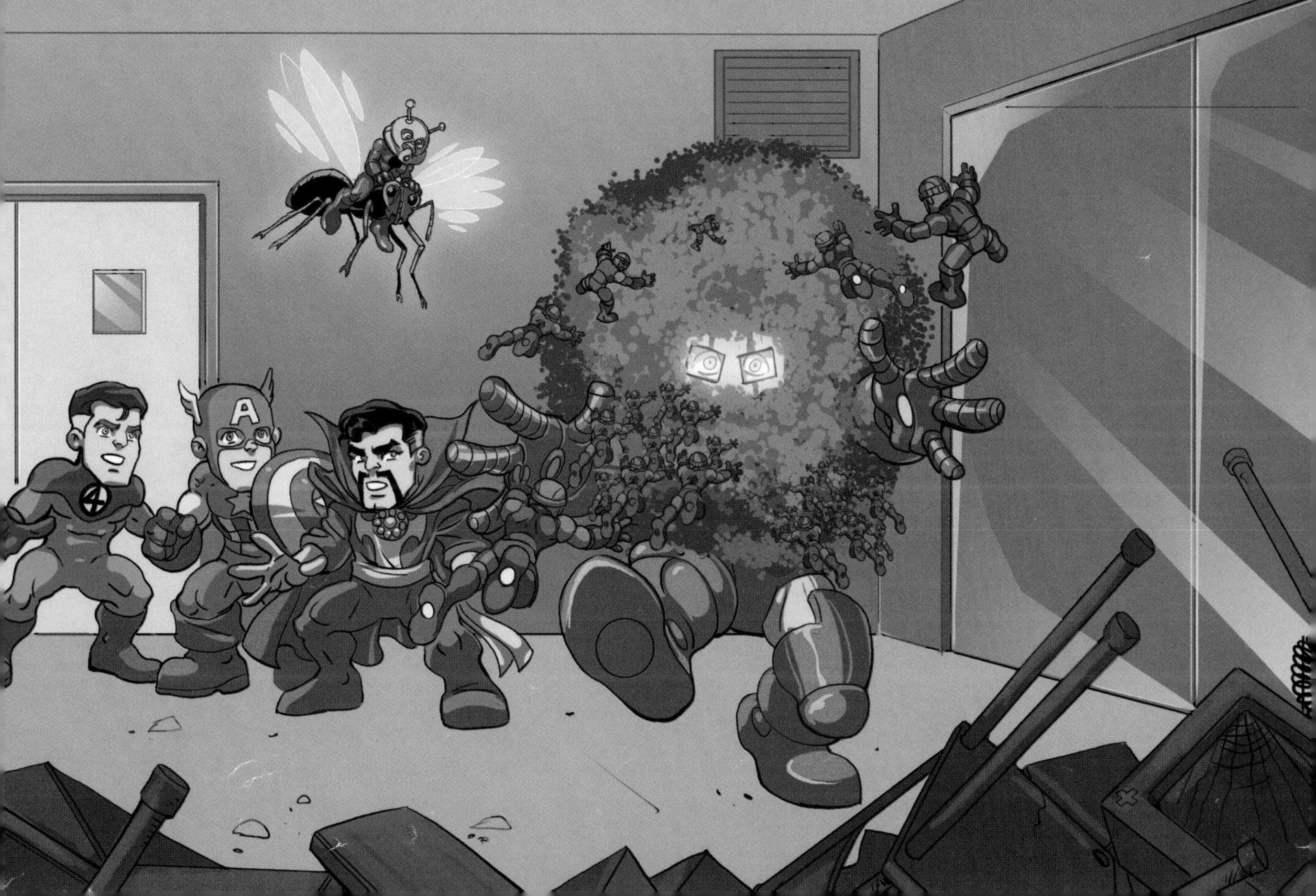

“Just slowly walk forward until I say stop,” Captain America tells Iron Man as he directs him into the medical lab’s isolation chamber. Mr. Fantastic closes the door behind Iron Man and the swarm of Sentinels.

“That should hold them,” Mr. Fantastic says.

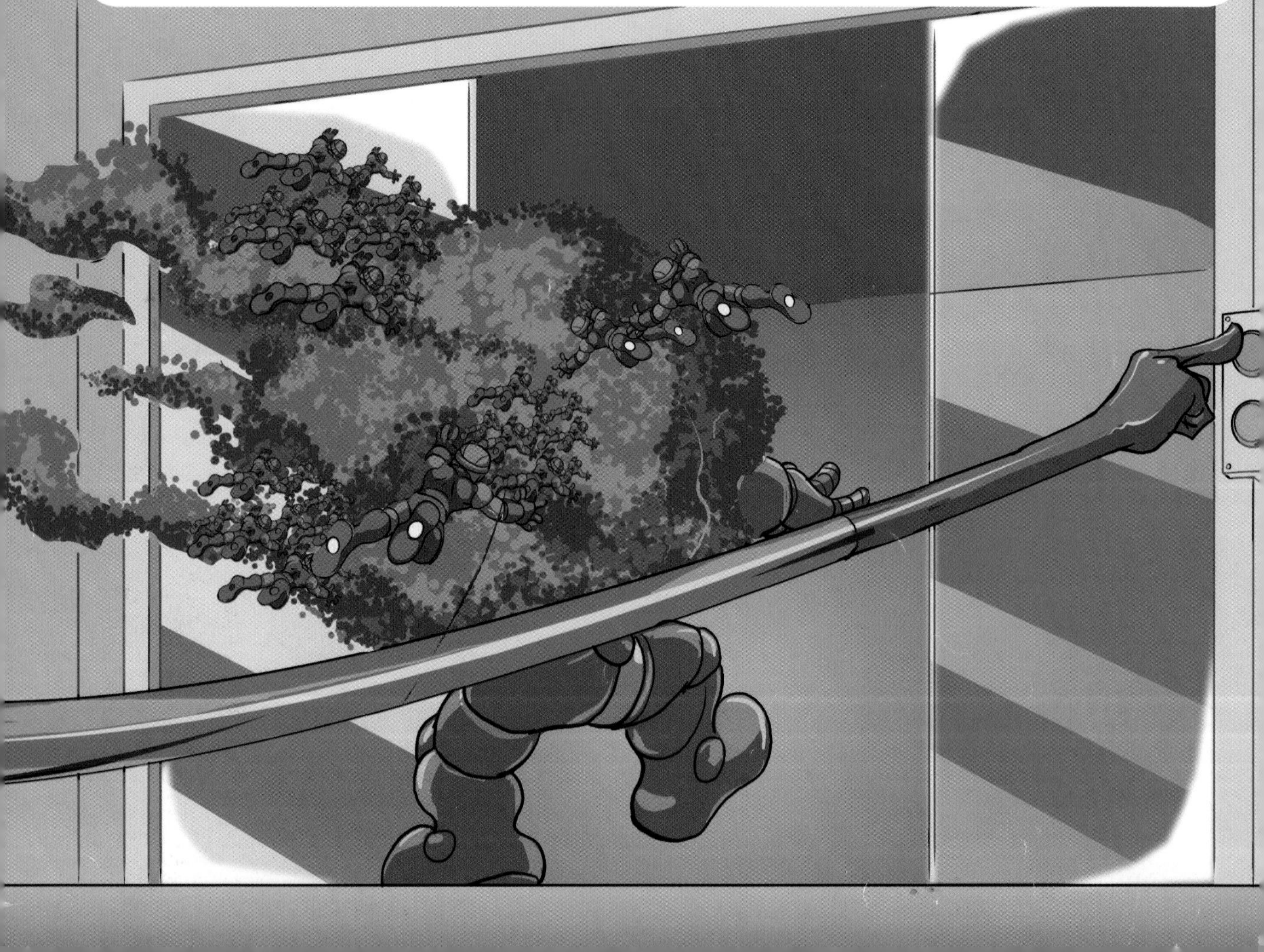

“Wait! Don’t leave me in here with them!” cries Iron Man. “I think they are trying to get into my suit!”

The rest of the Squad burst into laughter at the thought.

“Don’t worry. Strange and I will get them off you in just a minute,” reassures Mr. Fantastic.

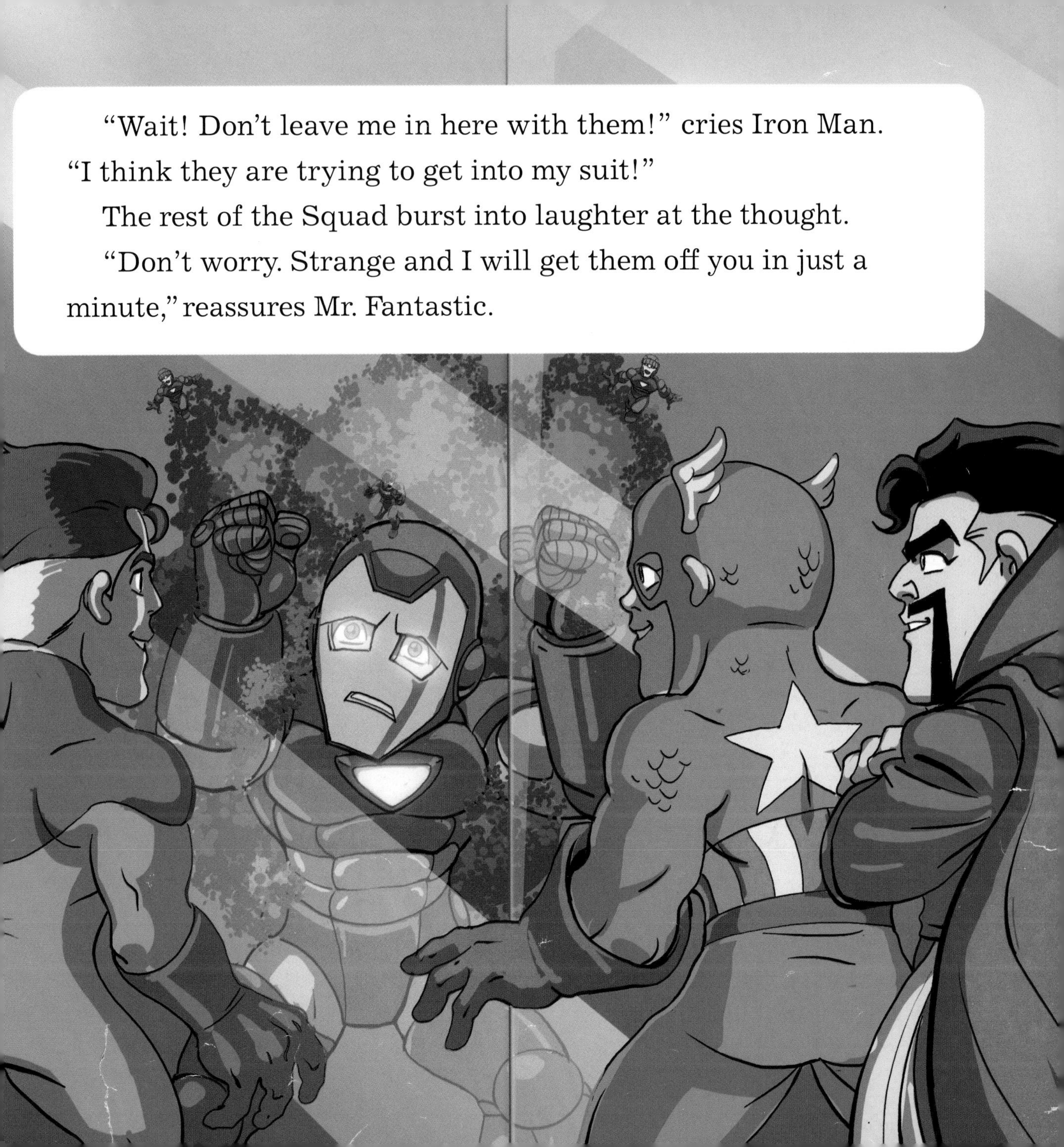

Suddenly, Hulk bursts through the door and hugs Dr. Strange.

"Hulk no sick! Doctor fix Hulk!" bellows the oversize hero. "Hulk love Doctor!"

Dr. Strange struggles to breathe in the grasp of the strongest member of the Super Hero Squad. "Well," he gasps, "at least something worked right today!"

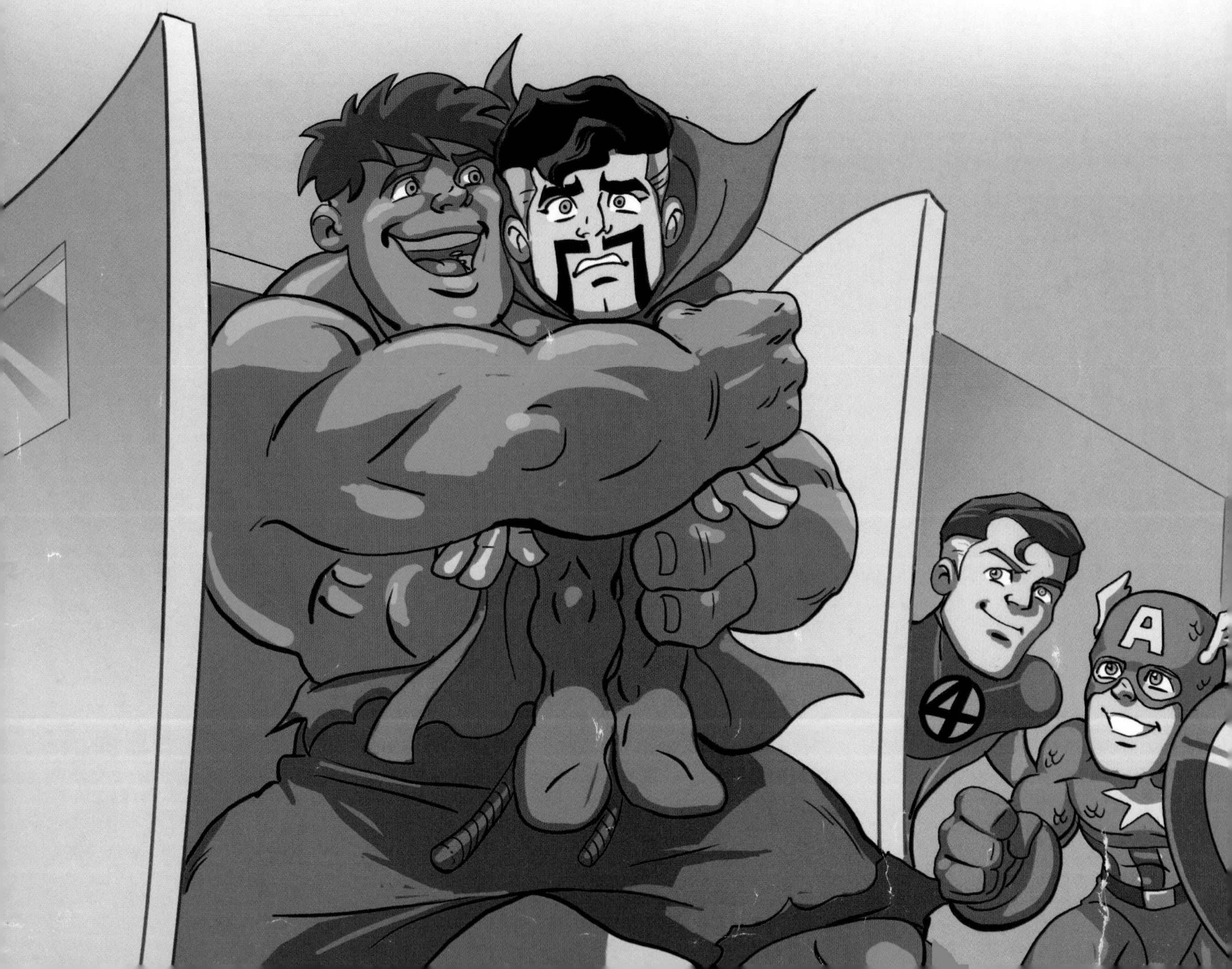
A
4

552(00